Rookie reader

Sam's Pet

BY CHARNAN SIMON

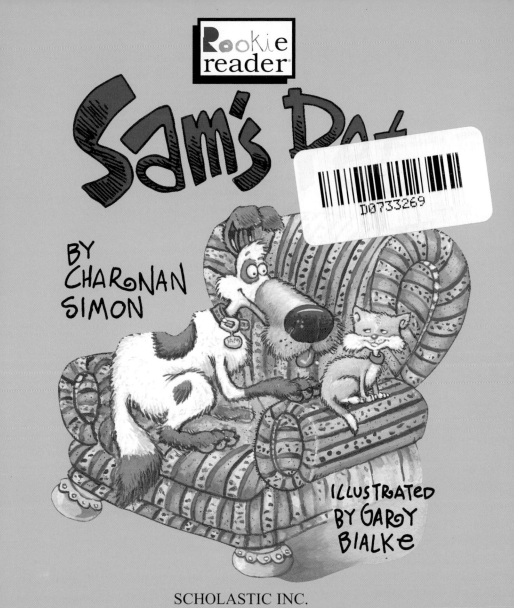

ILLUSTRATED BY GARY BIALKE

SCHOLASTIC INC.

New York Toronto London Auckland Sydney
Mexico City New Delhi Hong Kong Buenos Aires

To my Mom and Dad (who gave me Bootsie and Cookie) with love,
and to Lucy Wackman and the real Mabel.
—C.S.
For Jonesy, who sometimes still lets me
believe I'm the boss.
—G.B.

Reading Consultants
Linda Cornwell
Coordinator of School Quality And Professional Improvement
(Indiana State Teachers Association)

Katharine A. Kane
Education Consultant (Retired, San Diego County Office
of Education and San Diego State University)

ISBN 0-516-24174-5

12 11 10 9 8 7 6   5 6 7 8/0

Printed in the U.S.A.   61

First Scholastic printing, February 2003

Rosie and Sam had a new pet.

Mabel was tiny,

and adorable,

and dangerous.

Mabel did not want
to share Sam's food,

or his toys,

or his bed.

Next to Mabel,
Sam felt like a big, dumb dog.

One day, the neighborhood bully
came over to steal Sam's bone.

Sam never argued with Butch.

But Mabel did.

First she took care of Butch.

Then she took care of Sam.

Now Mabel loves
to share with Sam.

He's such a pussycat.

WORD LIST (54 WORDS)

a	did	new	she
adorable	dog	next	steal
and	dumb	not	such
argued	felt	now	the
bed	first	of	then
big	food	one	tiny
bone	had	or	to
bully	he's	over	took
but	his	pet	toys
Butch	like	pussycat	want
came	loves	Rosie	was
care	Mabel	Sam	with
dangerous	neighborhood	Sam's	
day	never	share	

ABOUT THE AUTHOR

Charnan Simon lives in Madison, Wisconsin, with her husband, Tom, and her daughters, Ariel and Hana. She also lives with the real Sam, who is part collie and part golden retriever, and who would just love to have a kitten for a pet.

ABOUT THE ILLUSTRATOR

Gary Bialke is a medium-sized hound known mainly for his large bark and small bite. With a good disposition and outgoing personality, he prefers to see the waterbowl as half full even when it's half empty. He's considering getting a larger bowl.